THE ADVENTURE FRIENDS

Treasure Map

Read more books in
THE ADVENTURE FRIENDS series!

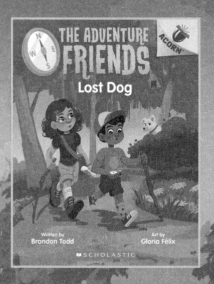

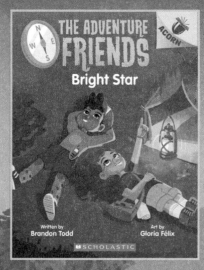

THE ADVENTURE FRIENDS

Treasure Map

WRITTEN BY
Brandon Todd

ART BY
Gloria Félix

ACORN™
SCHOLASTIC INC.

For Micah and all the adventures life brings.
—BT

For Francisco, Mochi, and all my adventure friends.
—GF

Text copyright © 2023 by Brandon Todd
Illustrations copyright © 2023 by Gloria Félix

Library of Congress Cataloging-in-Publication Data
Names: Todd, Brandon, author.
Title: Treasure map / Brandon Todd.
Description: New York: Scholastic, Inc., 2023. | Series: The adventure friends ; 1 | Audience: Ages 5–7. | Audience: Grades K–2. | Summary: Clarke is a girl who has just moved in and she is very serious about adventure; Miguel knows the neighborhood and is eager to meet new people and have adventures—so with walkie-talkies, a compass, paper, and colored pencils they set out to explore and draw an "adventure map"—or perhaps it is a treasure map as Miguel insists.
Identifiers: LCCN 2021021433 (print) |
ISBN 9781338805819 (paperback) | ISBN 9781338805826 (library binding) |
Subjects: LCSH: Cartography—Juvenile fiction. | Maps—Juvenile fiction. | Friendship—Juvenile fiction. | Picture books for children. | CYAC: Cartography—Fiction | Maps—Fiction. | Friendship—Fiction. | LCGFT: Picture books.
Classification: LCC PZ7.1.T6125 Tr 2023 (print) | LCC PZ7.1.T6125 (ebook) | DDC [E]—dc23
LC record available at https://lccn.loc.gov/2021021433
LC ebook record available at https://lccn.loc.gov/2021021434

10 9 8 7 6 5 4 3   24 25 26 27 28

Printed in the U.S.A.   40
First printing, January 2023
Edited by Katie Carella
Art direction by Brian LaRossa
Book design by Jaime Lucero

TABLE OF CONTENTS

MEET THE CHARACTERS

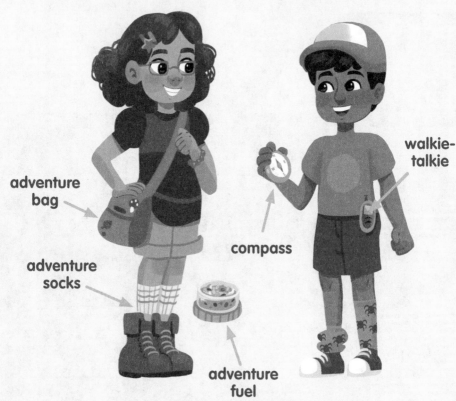

adventure bag

walkie-talkie

adventure socks

compass

adventure fuel
(This is what Clarke calls her mom's trail mix!)

Clarke
New to town.
Loves planning, drawing,
and ADVENTURE!

Miguel
Knows everyone in town.
Loves bugs, surprises,
and ADVENTURE!

WELCOME TO THE NEIGHBORHOOD

Miguel sat at his window.
A moving truck sat in front of
an empty house.

"New neighbors!" said Miguel.

Miguel loved meeting new people.
He ran outside to greet
his new neighbor.

"Hi! I'm Miguel," said Miguel. "I like
your bag. What's your name?"

"Clarke," replied Clarke. "And this is not
just a bag. It is my **adventure bag**."

"Cool!" said Miguel.

"Thanks," said Clarke. "Do you like adventures too?"

"Roger that," said Miguel. "That is walkie-talkie for 'yep.' Now we can say cool stuff to each other, like 'over and out.' That's walkie-talkie for 'I'm done talking.'"

The walkie-talkie was a very good gift.
Clarke wanted to give Miguel a gift too.

She found the perfect thing
in her **adventure bag**.

"You'll need this on our adventures,"
said Clarke.

"VERY COOL!" said Miguel.

He looked at the round object
in his hand. It had a red-and-blue
needle that spun around and four letters:
N, E, S, W.

"What is it?" he asked.

"A compass," said Clarke. "The red end
of the needle always points NORTH.
If you line it up with the N,
it will lead you home."

Miguel lined up the red end of the
needle with the N. Then he walked in
the direction it pointed.

Before he knew it, he was in his front yard!

"The compass works!" said Miguel over his walkie-talkie.

He waved to Clarke.

"The walkie-talkies work too!" said Clarke. "Let's go exploring soon."

"Roger that," said Miguel. "Over and out."

THE ADVENTURE MAP

Clarke put on her **adventure socks**.
She packed her **adventure bag**.
It was time to go exploring.

"Miguel. Come in, Miguel.
Are you ready for our first adventure?"
Clarke called over her walkie-talkie.

"Roger that!" Miguel replied.

"Bring your compass," said Clarke.
"Over and out."

Miguel met Clarke in her front yard.

"I need to know how to get around my new neighborhood," said Clarke. "So today's mission is to make a map."

"Like a treasure map?!" asked Miguel.

"No," said Clarke. "This will be an **adventure map**."

Clarke opened her **adventure bag**.
She pulled out colored pencils
and a pad of paper.

"We will start here. See? This is
my house," said Clarke.

"Put mine on there too," said Miguel.
"NORTH of your house!"

Clarke added a house right above hers.

"Now let's use your compass. Which direction should we go?" asked Clarke.

Miguel looked down at his compass. He still wasn't sure what the other three letters meant.

"Let's go toward the w," Clarke decided.

Miguel lined up the red end of the needle with the N. Then he walked in the direction of the w.

19

"Wow! We found a river!" shouted Clarke.

"Aha!" said Miguel. "Now I get it! The **w** is for 'water.'"

"No," said Clarke, giggling. "w means WEST. E is for EAST, and s is for SOUTH."

Clarke added wavy lines to the left of their houses on the map.

"We should go in all the directions.
So you can fill your map," said Miguel.

To the **SOUTH**, they found a church
and a market.

To the **EAST**, they found a school
and a park.

Clarke added each new location to her map.

Just as he feared, NORTH led them
back home and to the end
of their adventure.

THE TREASURE MAP

The next morning, Miguel got on the walkie-talkie.

"Let's go find treasure," said Miguel. "Meet me at the park and bring the treasure map. Over and out."

"It's not a treasure map," said Clarke.

But Miguel didn't hear her.
He was already halfway to the park.

Clarke grabbed the
adventure map.

She put on her
adventure socks.

And she headed out.

Clarke met Miguel at the park gate.

"This park is HUGE," said Miguel.
"There has to be treasure here."

Clarke took out her colored pencils.
"Where should we look first?"

Miguel took out his compass.
"Let's go WEST!" he said.

"We found a pond!" shouted Clarke.

"Are you sure **w** doesn't stand for 'water'?" asked Miguel.

Clarke smiled and added a blue circle to her map.

The two explorers searched the pond.
No treasure.

They searched the gazebo
and the playground.

They even searched a
creepy-looking tree.

No treasure.

Then they found a sand pit.

"Buried treasure!" said Miguel.

They dug and dug and dug.

Still no
treasure.

"I need a break," said Clarke.
"Do you want a snack?"

She offered some **adventure fuel**
to Miguel.

As they sat, they looked over the map.

"This map does kind of look like a treasure map," Clarke said. "It just needs an **X**."

That gave Miguel an idea.

"I know where the treasure is!" shouted Miguel.

He jumped up and took off running. He ran **EAST**, toward a blank spot on the map.

Clarke chased
after him.

Miguel stopped at the old train tracks.

"There is treasure here! I'm sure of it," he said.

Clarke searched the tracks.

She found three pennies and one nickel.

"**X** marks the spot!" replied Miguel.

He pointed to the railroad-crossing sign.

Clarke added an **X** to her map.

"See, it really was a treasure map,"
said Miguel.

OVER AND OUT

"We need cool code names for when we use our walkie-talkies," said Miguel.

"My code name could be Dung Beetle," he said.

"Gross!" Clarke laughed.

Then she thought of the coolest name she could.

"My code name is Thunder Walrus," Clarke said.

"Whoa!" said Miguel. "You are good
at code names."

"Come on, Dung Beetle," said Clarke.
"We should get home."

"I am rethinking my code name,"
said Miguel. "Mine stinks."

They started home, following their map.

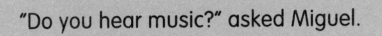
"Do you hear music?" asked Miguel.

"Yeah. Where is it coming from?" asked Clarke.

45

The music got louder as they walked.

Then they stopped.

Clarke's and Miguel's eyes got wide.
"ICE CREAM!" they both screamed.

They ran over to the ice cream truck.

Clarke read through all the flavors.

Miguel and the ice cream man chatted. He showed the man the treasure from the park.

Then Miguel traded their treasure
for two large ice cream cones.

Clarke was amazed. "Two cones for eight
cents?! You are really good at trades."

Miguel shrugged.
"The ice cream man loves treasure."

Clarke smiled and added the
ice cream truck to her map.

The map was complete. The ice cream was gone. The adventure was over.

Clarke took off her **adventure socks**.

Then she taped her **adventure map** to the wall.

Clarke's walkie-talkie buzzed.

"Come in, Thunder Walrus. Are you there?" said Miguel.

"Roger that," said Clarke.

"I came up with a new code name: Captain Compass," said Miguel.

"It's perfect," said Clarke.

"I am glad I found an **adventure friend**," she said.

"Me too," said Miguel. "Over and out."

ABOUT THE CREATORS

Brandon Todd lives in North Kansas City, Missouri. When he was a kid, he made treasure maps of the woods by his house. The biggest treasure he found was three golf balls! He is the author and illustrator of a picture book called TOU-CAN'T!: A LITTLE SISTER STORY. The Adventure Friends is his first early reader series.

Gloria Félix was born and raised in Uruapan, a city in Michoacán, Mexico. This beautiful, small city is one of her biggest inspirations when it comes to her art. In addition to children's books, Gloria makes art for the animation industry. Her hobbies include walking, life drawing, and plein-air painting with her friends. Currently, she lives and paints in Guadalajara.

YOU CAN DRAW CLARKE!

1 Draw the outline of Clarke's head, shirt, and shorts.

2 Draw the outline of her hair, arms, and legs. Add details to her hands.

3 Draw her bag. Add details to her legs, socks, and boots.

4 Draw Clarke's face. Add details to her shirt, shorts, and bag.

5 Add two hair clips and one bracelet. Don't forget her glasses!

6 Color in your drawing!

WHAT'S YOUR STORY?

Clarke and Miguel make a map and find treasure.
Imagine **you** make a map. Where would it lead?
What locations would be found on your map?
Who would you take on your adventure?
Write and draw your story!